For Michael and James

Carolrhoda Books
A division of Lerner Publishing Group, Inc.
241 First Avenue North
Minneapolis, MN 55401 U.S.A.

Website address: www.lernerbooks.com

Kulka, Joe.
    Wolf's coming! / by Joe Kulka.
        p.   cm.
    Summary: All of the animals in the forest go into hiding because the
wolf is coming, but why they are hiding is the big surprise.
    ISBN-13: 978-1-57505-930-3 (lib. bdg. : alk. paper)
    ISBN-10: 1-57505-930-4 (lib. bdg. : alk. paper)
    1. Children's poetry, American.   2. Birthdays—Juvenile literature.
    I. Title.
PS3611.U435W65 2007
811'.6—dc22   2006013865

Manufactured in the United States of America
3 4 5 6 . 7 8 – JR – 13 12 11 10 09 08

WOLF'S COMING!

JOE KULKA

CAROLRHODA BOOKS MINNEAPOLIS • NEW YORK

A distant howl rides the breeze,
echoing through all the trees.

Hurry, HURRY!
Don't be slow!
Follow me.
C'mon, let's go!

A shadowy figure climbs the hill,
getting close and closer still.

Faster, FASTER!
Take my hand!
Run back home
like we planned.

Shadows lengthen. It's getting late.
The wolf is NOW outside the gate.

Quickly! QUICKLY!
Get inside!
Shut the door,
better hide.

The moonlight shines on his fangs.
His belly growls with hunger pangs.

Closer, CLOSER.
Next to me.
Pull the shade
so he can't see.

WOLF'S COMING!

Glowing ember eyes appear.
Pointed ears strain to hear.

Hush now, HUSH NOW.
Not a peep.
You must be still,
like you're asleep.

WOLF'S HERE!

The front door opens with a creak.
The big wolf leans in for a peek.

Tightly, TIGHTLY,
shut your eyes.
With all your might yell . . .

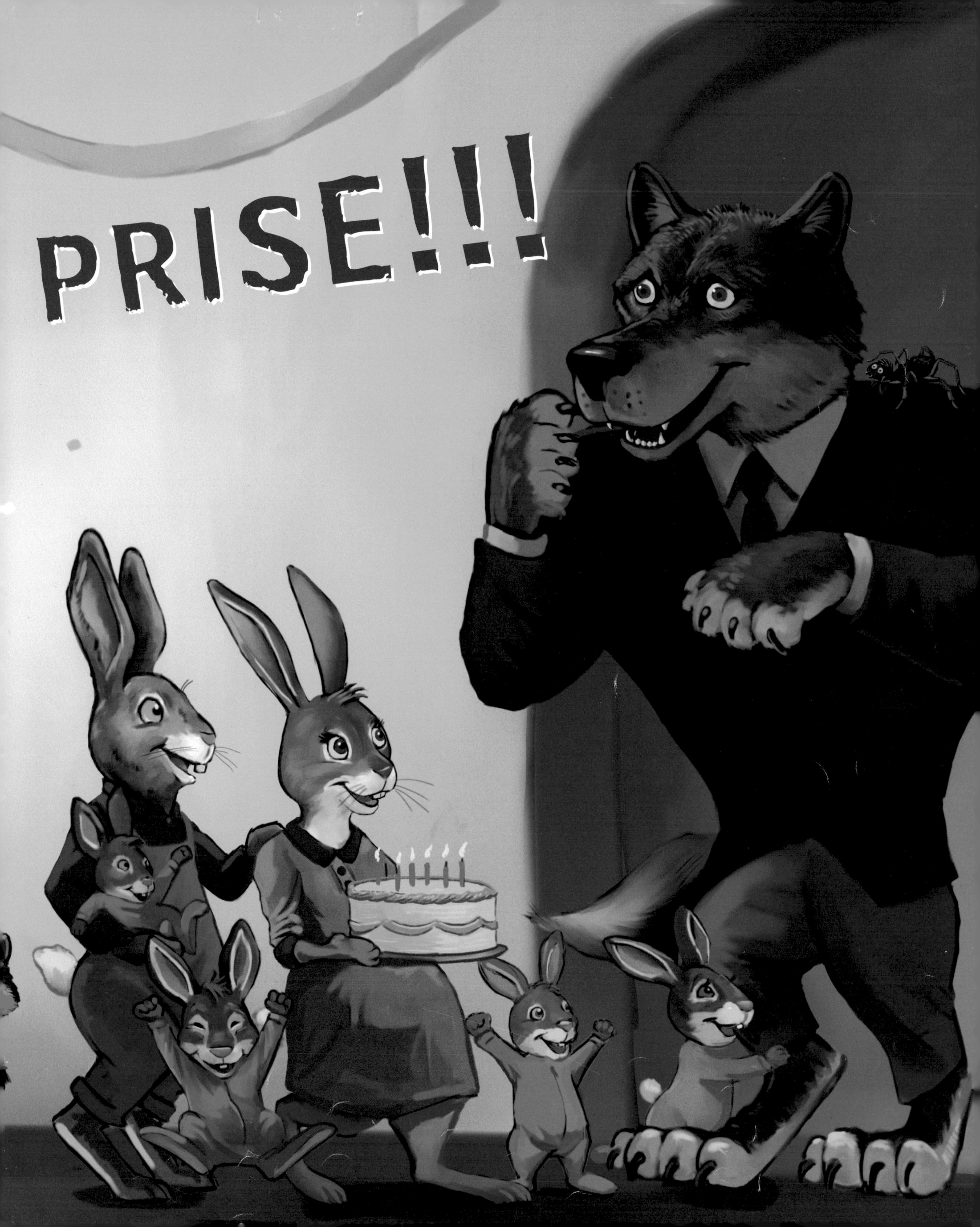
PRISE!!!

Laughing, LAUGHING!
So much fun!
Cake and pizza for everyone!

HAPPY BIRTHDAY, WOLF!